Praise for *Gone Girl*

'Flynn, an extraordinarily good writer, plays her readers with the finesse and delicacy of an expert angler . . . an absolute must-read' *Observer*

'These voices are wonderfully authentic, to the point where the reader becomes a gawker at the full-spectrum of marital dysfunction. Excellent'

Guardian

'Flynn keeps the accelerator firmly to the floor, ratcheting up the tension with wildly unexpected plot twists, contradictory stories and the tantalising feeling that nothing is as it seems. Deviously good' *Marie Claire*

'*Gone Girl* is superbly constructed, ingeniously paced and absolutely terrifying . . . a five-star suspense mystery' A. N. Wilson, *Reader's Digest*

'A chilling, stylish read about another unknowable woman' *Elle*

'Read it and stay single' *Financial Times*

'Flynn is a brilliantly accomplished psychological crime writer and this latest book is so dark, so twisted and so utterly compelling that it actually messes with your mind' *Daily Mail*

'Nothing's as it seems – Flynn is a fabulous plotter, and a very sharp observer of modern life'

Kate Saunders, *The Times*

'Immensely dark and deeply intelligent, *Gone Girl* is a book about how well one person can truly know another' *Metro*

'Smart, suspenseful and brilliantly written, *Gone Girl* is a class act' *Independent*

'Exhilarating and creepy, it has sent me rushing off to her other novels' *New Statesman*

'A near-masterpiece. Flynn is an extraordinary writer who, with every sentence, makes words do things that other writers merely dream of'

Sophie Hannah, *Sunday Express*

Praise for *Dark Places*

'Gillian Flynn is the real deal, a sharp, acerbic, and compelling storyteller with a knack for the macabre' Stephen King

'Gillian Flynn's writing is compulsively good. I would rather read her than just about any other crime writer' Kate Atkinson

'With her blistering debut *Sharp Objects*, Gillian Flynn hit the ground running. *Dark Places* demonstrates that was no fluke' Val McDermid

'Gutsy, atmospheric and suspense-loaded'
Fanny Blake, *Woman & Home*

'I don't think I'll read a better thriller this year'
Alex Heminsley, BBC 6 Music

'This is only Flynn's second crime novel . . . and demonstrates even more forcibly her precocious writing ability and talent for the macabre'
Daily Mail

Praise for *Sharp Objects*

'To say this is a terrific debut novel is really too mild . . . [it is] a relentlessly creepy family saga. I found myself dreading the last thirty pages or so, but was helpless to stop turning them. Then, after the lights were out, the story just stayed there in my head, coiled and hissing, like a snake in a cave'
Stephen King

'A stylish and compelling debut. A real winner'
Harlan Coben

'It is a stunningly accomplished evocation of the oppressiveness of small-town life and is just as assured in depicting the gradually revealed psychological disorder that links Camille to both killer and victims' *Sunday Times*

'Relentless, often creepy, but never less than real, this stylish and gripping tale will give you the shivers' *Guardian*

'Compulsively disturbing' *Time Out*

'[A] striking first novel . . . a relentlessly dark tale, with some very disturbed characters'

Sunday Telegraph

'[A] sinister and stylish psychological drama . . . Flynn brilliantly depicts the lurking malice and secrets of a small community as well as reminding us how scary teenage girls can be' *Daily Mail*

'This is a stylish thriller about housewives who don't recognise their own desperations, while the reader recognises with fascinated clarity the nastiness and vacuity of life in an updated Stepford'

Literary Review

Gillian Flynn is the bestselling author of three novels, including the international phenomenon *Gone Girl*. Her first novel, *Sharp Objects*, was the winner of two CWA Daggers and was shortlisted for the Gold Dagger, and her second, *Dark Places*, has been adapted into a film starring Charlize Theron. *Gone Girl* was a massive No. 1 bestseller, with over 10 million sales worldwide, and was made into a critically-acclaimed, smash-hit film by David Fincher, starring Ben Affleck and Rosamund Pike. The screenplay was written by Gillian and was nominated for a Golden Globe and a Bafta. *The Grownup* won the Edgar Award for Best Short Story in 2015.

Also by Gillian Flynn

SHARP OBJECTS
DARK PLACES
GONE GIRL

THE GROWNUP

GILLIAN FLYNN

A STORY BY THE AUTHOR OF GONE GIRL

WEIDENFELD & NICOLSON

First published as *The Grownup* in Great Britain
by Weidenfeld & Nicolson in 2015
An imprint of the Orion Publishing Group Ltd
Carmelite House, 50 Victoria Embankment
London EC4Y 0DZ

An Hachette UK Company

1 3 5 7 9 10 8 6 4 2

This title was originally published in the anthology *Rogues*,
edited by George R.R. Martin and Gardner Dozois,
by Bantam Books, an imprint of Random House,
a division of Penguin Random House LLC in 2014.

A CIP catalogue record for this book
is available from the British Library.

ISBN 978 1 4746 0304 1

Printed in Great Britain by Clays Ltd, St Ives plc

The Orion Publishing Group's policy is to use papers that
are natural, renewable and recyclable products and made
from wood grown in sustainable forests. The logging and
manufacturing processes are expected to conform to the
environmental regulations of the country of origin.

www.orionbooks.co.uk

To David and Ceán, you sick, sick people.

I didn't stop giving hand jobs because I wasn't good at it. I stopped giving hand jobs because I was the best at it.

For three years, I gave the best hand job in the tristate area. The key is to not overthink it. If you start worrying about technique, if you begin analyzing rhythm and pressure, you lose the essential nature of the act. You have to mentally prepare beforehand, and then you have to stop thinking and trust your body to take over.

Basically, it's like a golf swing.

I jacked men off six days a week, eight hours a day, with a break for lunch, and I was always fully booked. I took two weeks of vacation every year, and I never worked holidays, because holiday hand jobs are sad for everyone. So over three years, I'm estimating that comes to about 23,546 hand jobs. So don't listen to that bitch Shardelle when she says I quit because I didn't have the talent.

I quit because when you give 23,546 hand jobs over a three-year period, carpal tunnel syndrome is a very real thing.

I came to my occupation honestly. Maybe "naturally" is the better word. I've never done much honestly in my life. I was raised in the city by a one-eyed mother (the opening line of my memoir), and she was not a nice lady. She didn't have a drug problem or a drinking problem, but she did have a working problem. She was the laziest bitch I ever met. Twice a week, we'd hit the streets downtown and beg. But because my mom hated being upright, she wanted to be strategic about the whole thing. Get as much money in as little time possible, and then go home and eat Zebra Cakes and watch arbitration-based reality court TV on our broken mattress amongst the stains. (That's what I remember most about my childhood: stains. I couldn't tell you the color of my mom's eye, but I could tell you the stain on the shag carpet was a deep, soupy brown, and the stains on the ceiling were burnt orange and the stains on the wall were a vibrant hungover-piss yellow.)

My mom and I would dress the part. She had a pretty, faded cotton dress, threadbare but screaming of decency. She put me in whatever I'd grown out of. We'd sit on a bench and target the right people to beg off. It's a fairly simple scheme. First choice is an out-of-town church bus. In-town church people, they'll just send you to the church. Out of town, they usually have to help, especially a one-eyed lady with a sad-faced kid. Second choice is women in sets of two. (Solo women can dart away too quickly; a pack of women is too hard to wrangle.) Third choice is a single woman who has that open look. You know it: The same woman you stop to ask for directions or the time of day, that's the woman we ask for money. Also youngish men with beards or guitars. Don't stop men in suits: That cliché is right, they're all assholes. Also skip the thumb rings. I don't know what it is, but men with thumb rings never help.

The ones we picked? We didn't call them marks, or prey or victims. We called them Tonys, because my dad was named Tony and he could never say no to anyone (although I assume he said no to my mom at least once, when she asked him to stay).

Once you stop a Tony, you can figure out in two seconds which way to beg. Some want it over with fast, like a mugging. You blurt. "Weneed-moneyforfoodyouhaveanychange?" Some want to luxuriate in your misfortune. They'll only give you money if you give them something to feel better about, and the sadder your story, the better they feel about helping you, and the more money you get. I'm not blaming them. You go to the theater, you want to be entertained.

My mom had grown up on a farm downstate.

Her own mother died in childbirth; her daddy grew soy and raised her when he wasn't too exhausted. She came up here for college, but her daddy got cancer, and the farm got sold, and ends stopped meeting, and she had to drop out. She worked as a waitress for three years, but then her little girl came along, and her little girl's daddy left, and before you knew it . . . she was one of them. The needy. She was not proud . . .

You get the idea. That was just the starter story. You can go from there. You can tell real quick if the person wants a scrappy, up-by-the-bootstraps tale: Then I was suddenly an honor-roll student at a distant charter school (I was, but the truth isn't the point here), and Mom just needed gas money to get me there (I actually took three buses on my own). Or if the person wants a damn-the-system story: Then I was immediately afflicted by some rare disease (named after whatever asshole my mom was dating—Todd-Tychon Syndrome, Gregory-Fisher Disease), and my healthcare woes had left us broke.

My mom was sly but lazy. I was much more
ambitious. I had lots of stamina and no pride. By
the time I was thirteen, I was outbegging her
by hundreds of dollars a day, and by the time I was
sixteen, I'd left her and the stains and the TV—
and, yes, high school—and struck out on my own.
I'd go out each morning and beg for six hours. I
knew who to approach and for how long and
exactly what to say. I was never ashamed. What I
did was purely transactional: You made someone
feel good and they gave you money.

So you can see why the whole hand-job thing
felt like a natural career progression.

Spiritual Palms (I didn't name the place, don't
blame me) was in a tony neighborhood to the west
of downtown. Tarot cards and crystal balls up
front, illegal soft-core sex work in back. I'd
answered an ad for a receptionist. It turned out
"receptionist" meant "hooker." My boss Viveca is
a former receptionist and current bona fide palm
reader. (Although Viveca isn't her bona fide name,
her bona fide name is Jennifer, but people don't

believe Jennifers can tell the future; Jennifers can tell you which cute shoes to buy or what farmer's market to visit, but they should keep their hands off other people's futures.) Viveca employs a few fortune-tellers up front and runs a tidy little room in back. The room in back looks like a doctor's office: It has paper towels and disinfectant and an exam table. The girls froofed it up with scarves draped over lamps and potpourri and sequined pillows—all this stuff only girly-girls would possibly care about. I mean, if I were a guy, looking to pay a girl to wank me off, I wouldn't walk in the room and say, "My God, I smell hints of fresh strudel and nutmeg . . . quick, grab my dick!" I'd walk in a room and say very little, which is what most of them do.

He's unique, the man who comes in for a hand job. (And we only do hand jobs here, or at least I only do hand jobs—I have an arrest record for a few petty thefts, dumb stuff I did at eighteen, nineteen, twenty, that will ensure I never ever *ever* get a decent job, and so I don't need to pile a serious prostie bust on top of it.) A hand-job guy is a very different creature from a guy who wants a blow job or a guy who wants sex. Sure, for some men, a hand job is just a gateway sex act. But I had a lot of repeat customers: They will never want more than a hand job. They don't consider a hand job cheating. Or else they worry about disease, or else they never have the courage to ask for more. They tend to be tense, nervous married men, men with midlevel, mostly powerless jobs. I'm not judging, I'm just giving my assessment. They want you attractive but not slutty. For instance, in my real life I wear glasses, but I don't when I'm in back because it's distracting—they think you're going to pull a Sexy Librarian act on them, and it makes them tense while they wait for the first chords of a ZZ Top song and then they don't hear it and they get embarrassed for thinking that you were going to do Sexy Librarian and then they're distracted and the whole thing takes longer than anyone wants.

They want you friendly and pleasant but not

weak. They don't want to feel like predators. They want this transactional. Service-oriented. So you exchange some polite conversation about the weather and a sports team they like. I usually try to find some sort of inside joke we can repeat each visit—an inside joke is like a symbol of friendship without having to do the work required of an actual friendship. So you say, *I see the strawberries are in season!* or *We need a bigger boat* (these are actual inside jokes I'm giving you), and then the ice is broken and they don't feel like they're scumbags because you're friends, and then the mood is set and you can get to it.

When people ask me that question that everyone asks: "What do you do?" I'd say, "I'm in customer service," which was true. To me, it's a nice day's work when you make a lot of people smile. I know that sounds too earnest, but it's true. I mean, I would rather be a librarian, but I worry about the job security. Books may be temporary; dicks are forever.

The problem was, my wrist was killing me.

Barely thirty and I had the wrist of an octogenarian and an unsexy athletic brace to match. I took it off before jobs but that Velcro-rip sound made men a little edgy. One day, Viveca visited me in back. She's a heavy woman, like an octopus—lots of beads and ruffles and scarves floating around her, along with the big scent of cologne. She has hair dyed the color of fruit punch and insists it's real. (*Viveca: Grew up the youngest child in a working-class family; indulgent of people she likes; cries at commercials; multiple failed attempts to be a vegetarian.* Just my guess.)

"Are you clairvoyant, Nerdy?" she asked. She called me Nerdy because I wore glasses and read books and ate yogurt on my lunch break. I'm not really a nerd; I only aspire to be one. Because of the high-school-dropout thing, I'm a self-didact. (Not a dirty word, look it up.) I read constantly. I think. But I lack formal education. So I'm left with the feeling that I'm smarter than everyone around me but that if I ever got around really smart people—people who went to universities and drank wine and spoke Latin—that they'd be bored as hell by me. It's a lonely way to go through life. So I wear the name as a badge of honor. That someday I may not totally bore some really smart people. The question is: How do you find smart people?

"Clairvoyant? No."

"A seer? You ever had visions?"

"No." I thought the whole fortune-telling crap was *fer the berds*, as my mom would say. She really was from a farm downstate, that part was true.

Viveca stopped fiddling with one of her beads.

"Nerdy, I'm trying to help you here."

I got it. I'm not usually that slow, but my wrist was throbbing. That distracting kind of pain where all you can think about is how to stop the pain. Also, in my defense, Viveca usually only asks questions so she can talk—she doesn't really care about your answers.

"Whenever I meet someone, I have this immediate vision," I said, in her plummy, wise voice. "Of who they are and what they need. I can see it like a color, a halo, around them." This was all actually true but the last part.

"You see auras." She smiled. "I knew you did."

That's how I found out I was moving up front. I would read auras, which meant I needed zero training. "Just tell them what they want to hear," Viveca said. "Work 'em like a rib." And when people asked me: "What do you do?" I'd say, "I'm a vision specialist," or "I'm in therapeutic practices." Which was true.

The fortune-teller clients were almost all women, and the hand-job clients were obviously all men, so we ran the place like clockwork. It wasn't a big space: You had to get a guy in and settled in the back room, and make sure he was coming right before the woman was ushered into her appointment. You didn't want any orgasm yelps from the back when a lady was telling you how her marriage was coming apart. The new-puppy excuse only works once.

The whole thing was risky, in that Viveca's clients were mostly upper-middle class and lower-upper class. Being of these classes, they're easily offended. If sad, rich housewives don't want their fortunes told by a Jennifer, they definitely don't want them told by a diligent former sex worker with a bad wrist. Appearances are everything. These are not people who want to slum it. These are people whose primary purpose is to live in the city but feel like they're in the suburbs. Our front office looked like a Pottery Barn ad. I dressed accordingly, which is basically Funky Artist as approved of and packaged by Anthropologie. Peasant blouses, that's the key.

The women who came in groups, they were frivolous, fancy, boozy, ready to have fun. The ones who came alone, though, they wanted to believe. They were desperate, and they didn't have good enough insurance for a therapist. Or they didn't know they were desperate enough to need a therapist. It was hard to feel sorry for them. I tried to because you don't want your mystic, the keeper of your future, to roll her eyes at you. But I mean, come on. Big house in the city, husbands who didn't beat them and helped with the kids, sometimes with careers but always with book clubs. And still they felt sad. That's what they always ended up saying: "But I'm just sad." Feeling sad means having too much time on your hands, usually. Really. I'm not a licensed therapist but usually it means too much time.

So I say things like, "A great passion is about to enter your life." Then you pick something you can make them do. You figure out what will make them feel good about themselves. Mentor a child, volunteer at a library, neuter some dogs, go green. You don't say it as a suggestion though, that's the key. You say it as a warning. "A great passion is about to enter your life . . . you must tread carefully or it will eclipse everything else that matters to you!"

I'm not saying it's always that easy, but it's often that easy. People want passion. People want a sense of purpose. And when they get those things, then they come back to you because you predicted their future, and it was good.

Susan Burke was different. She seemed smarter from the second I saw her. I entered the room one rainy April morning, fresh from a hand-job client. I still kept a few, my longtime favorites, and so I had just been assisting a sweet dorky rich guy who called himself Michael Audley (I say "called" because I assume a rich guy wouldn't give me his real name). Mike Audley: *Overshadowed by jock brother; came into his own in college; extremely brainy but not smug about it; compulsive jogger*. Just my guess. The only thing I really knew about Mike was he loved books. He recommended books with the fervor I've always craved as an aspiring nerd: with urgency and camaraderie. You *have* to read this! Pretty soon we had our own private (occasionally sticky) book club. He was big into "Classic Stories of the Supernatural" and he wanted me to be too ("You are a *psychic* after all," he said with a smile). So that day we discussed the themes of loneliness and need in *The Haunting of*

Hill House, he came, I sani-wiped myself and grabbed his loaner for next time: *The Woman in White*. ("You *have* to read this! It's one of the all-time best.")

Then I tousled my hair to look more intuitive, straightened my peasant blouse, tucked the book under my arm, and ran out to the main room. Not quite clockwork: I was thirty-seven seconds late. Susan Burke was waiting; she shook my hand with a nervous, birdy up and down, and the repetitive motion made me wince. I dropped my book and we banged heads picking it up. Definitely not what you want from your psychic: a Three Stooges bit.

I motioned her to a seat. I put on my wise voice and asked her why she was here. That's the easiest way to tell people what they want: Ask them what they want.

Susan Burke was silent for a few beats. Then: "My life is falling apart," she murmured. She was extremely pretty but so wary and nervous you didn't realize she was pretty until you looked hard at her. Looked past the glasses to the bright blue eyes. Imagined the dull blond hair de-stringed. She was clearly rich. Her handbag was too plain to be anything but incredibly expensive. Her dress was mousy but well made. In fact, it could be the dress wasn't mousy—she just wore it that way. *Smart but not creative*, I thought. *Conformist. Lives in fear of saying or doing the wrong thing. Lacks confidence. Probably browbeaten by her parents, and now browbeaten by her husband. Husband has temper— her whole goal each day is to get to the end without a blowup. Sad. She'll be one of the sad ones.*

Susan Burke began sobbing then. She sobbed for a minute and a half. I was going to give her two minutes before I interrupted, but she stopped on her own.

"I don't know why I'm here," she said. She pulled a pastel handkerchief from her bag but didn't use it. "This is crazy. It just keeps getting worse."

I gave her my best *there, there* without touching her. "What's going on in your life?"

She wiped her eyes and stared at me a beat. Blinked. "Don't you know?"

Then she gave me a smile. Sense of humor. Unexpected.

"So how do we do this?" she asked, tucking herself in again. She massaged a spot near the nape of her neck. "How does this work?"

"I'm a psychological intuitive," I began. "Do you know what that means?"

"You can read people well."

"Yes, to a degree, but my powers are much stronger than just a hunch. All my senses play a part. I can feel vibrations coming off people. I can see auras. I can smell despair, or dishonesty, or depression. It's a gift I've had since I was a small child. My mother was a deeply depressed, unbalanced woman. A dark blue haze followed her. When she was near me, my skin plinked—like someone was playing a piano—and she smelled of despair, which presents itself to me as the scent of bread."

"*Bread?*" she said.

"That was just her scent, of a desperate soul."
I needed to pick a new *eau de sad girl*. Not dying
leaves, too obvious, but something earthy. Mush-
rooms? No, inelegant.

"Bread, that is so strange," she said.

People usually asked what their scent or aura
was. It was their first step to committing to the
game. Susan shifted uncomfortably. "I don't mean
to be rude," she said. "But . . . I think this isn't for
me."

I waited her out. Empathetic silence is one of
the most underused weapons in the world.

"OK," Susan said. She tucked her hair behind
both ears—thick diamond-scattered wedding
bands flashing like the Milky Way—and looked
ten years younger. I could picture her as a kid,
a bookworm maybe, pretty but shy. Demanding
parents. Straight As, always. "So what do you read
off me?"

"There's something going on in your house."

"I already told you that." I could feel the
desperation coming off her: to believe in me.

"No, you told me your life was falling apart. I'm saying it's something to do with your house. You have a husband, I sense a lot of discord: I see you surrounded by a sick green, like an egg yolk gone bad. Swirls of a healthy vibrant turquoise on the outer edges. That tells me you had something good and it went very bad. Yes?"

Obviously this was an easy guess, but I liked my color arrangement; it felt right.

She glared at me. I was hitting on something close to the bone.

"I feel the same vibrations off you as my mother: those sharp, high piano plinks. You're desperate, you're in exquisite pain. You're not sleeping."

The mention of insomnia was always risky but usually paid off. People in pain don't generally sleep well. Insomniacs are exquisitely grateful for people to recognize their weariness.

"No, no, I sleep eight hours," Susan said.

"It's not a genuine sleep. You have unsettling dreams. Maybe not nightmares, maybe you don't even remember them, but you wake up feeling worn, achy."

See, you can rescue most bad guesses. This woman was in her forties; people in their forties usually wake up feeling achy. I know that from commercials.

"You store the anxiety in your neck," I continued. "Also, you smell of peonies. A child. You have a child?"

If she didn't have a child, then I just say, "But you *want* one." And she can deny it—*I've never, ever even thought about having kids*—and I can insist, and pretty soon she leaves thinking it because very few women decide not to procreate without some doubts. It's an easy thought to seed. Except this one's smart.

"Yes. Well, two. A son and a stepson."

Stepson, go with the stepson.

"Something is wrong in your house. Is it your stepson?"

She stood up, fumbled through her well-constructed bag.

"How much do I owe you?"

I got one thing wrong. I thought I'd never see her again. But four days later Susan Burke was back. ("Can *things* have auras?" she asked. "Like, objects. Or a house?") And then three days later ("Do you believe in evil spirits? Is there such a thing, do you think?") and then the next day.

I was right about her, mostly. Overbearing, demanding parents, straight As, Ivy League, a degree that had something to do with business. I asked her the question: What do you do? She explained and explained about downsizing and restructuring and client intersects, and when I frowned, she got impatient and said, "I define and eliminate problems." Things with her husband were OK except when it came to the stepson. The Burkes had moved into the city the year before, and that's when the kid went from troubled to troubling.

"Miles was never a sweet boy," she said. "I'm the only mom he's known—I've been with his dad since he was four. But he's always been cold.

Introverted. He's just empty. I hate myself for saying that. I mean, introverted is fine. But in the past year, since the move . . . he's changed. Become more aggressive. He's so angry. So dark. Threatening. He scares me."

The kid was fifteen, and had just been forcibly relocated from the suburbs into the city where he didn't know anyone, and he was already an awkward, nerdy kid. Of course he was angry. That would have been helpful, my saying that, but I didn't. I seized an opportunity.

I'd been trying to move into the domestic aura-cleansing business. Basically when someone moves into a new home, they call you. You wander around the house burning sage and sprinkling salt and murmuring a lot. Fresh start, wipe away any lingering bad energy from previous owners. Now that people were moving back into the heart of the city, into all the old historic houses, it seemed like a boom industry waiting to happen. A hundred-year-old house, that's a lot of leftover vibes.

"Susan, have you considered that the house is affecting your son's behavior?"

Susan leaned in, her eyes wide. "Yes! Yes, I do. Is that crazy? That's why . . . why I came back. Because . . . there was blood on my wall."

"*Blood?*"

She leaned in and I could smell the mint masking sour breath. "Last week. I didn't want to say anything . . . I thought you'd think I was crazy. But it was there. One long trickle from the floor to the ceiling. Am I . . . am I crazy?"

I met her at the house the next week. Driving up her street in my trusty hatchback, I thought, *rust*. Not blood. Something from the walls, the roof. Who knew what old houses were built of? Who knew what could leak out after a hundred years? The question was how to play it. I really wasn't interested in getting into exorcism, demonology church shit. I don't think that's what Susan wanted either. But she did invite me to her house, and women like that don't invite over women like me unless they want something. Comfort. I would breeze over the "blood trickle," find an explanation for it, and yet still insist the house could use a cleansing.

Repeated cleansings. We had yet to discuss money. Twelve visits for $2,000 seemed like a good price point. Spread them out, one a month, over a year, and give the stepson time to sort himself out, get adjusted to the new school, the new kids. Then he's cured and I'm the hero, and pretty soon Susan is referring all her rich, nervous friends to me. I could go into business for myself, and when people asked me, "What do you do?" I'd say, *I'm an entrepreneur* in that haughty way entrepreneurs had. Maybe Susan and I would become friends. Maybe she'd invite me to a book club. I'd sit by a fire and nibble on Brie and say, *I'm a small business owner, an entrepreneur, if you will.* I parked, got out of the car, and took a big breath of optimistic spring air.

But then I spotted Susan's house. I actually stopped and stared. Then I shivered.

It was different from the rest.

It lurked. It was the only remaining Victorian

house in a long row of boxy new construction, and maybe that's why it seemed alive, calculating. The mansion's front was all elaborate, carved stone-work, dizzying in its detail: flowers and filigrees, dainty rods and swooping ribbons. Two life-sized angels framed the doorway, their arms reaching upward, their faces fascinated by something I couldn't see.

I watched the house. It watched me back through long, baleful windows so tall a child could stand in the sill. And one was. I could see the length of his thin body: gray trousers, black sweater, a maroon tie perfectly knotted at the neck. A thicket of dark hair covering his eyes. Then, a sudden blur, and he'd hopped down and disappeared behind the heavy brocade drapes.

The steps to the mansion were steep and long. My heart was thumping by the time I reached the top, passed the awestruck angels, reached the door, and rang the bell. As I waited I read the inscription carved in the stone near my feet.

CARTERHOOK MANOR
ESTABLISHED 1893
PATRICK CARTERHOOK

The carving was in a severe Victorian cursive, the two juicy o's dissected by a feathery curlicue. It made me want to protect my belly.

Susan opened the door with red eyes.

"Welcome to Carterhook Manor," she said, fake grandeur. She caught me staring—Susan never looked good when I saw her, but she hadn't even pretended to brush her hair, and a foul, acrid odor came off her. (Not "despair" or "depression," just bad breath and body odor.) She shrugged limply. "I've finally stopped sleeping."

The inside of the house was nothing like the outside. The interior had been gutted and now looked like every other rich person's house. It made me feel immediately more cheerful. I could cleanse *this* place: the tasteful recessed lights, the granite counters and stainless-steel appliances, the new, freakishly smooth wood paneling, wall upon wall of Botoxed oak.

"Let's start with the blood trickle," I suggested.

We climbed to the second floor. There were two more above it. The stairwell was open, and I peered up through the banisters to see a face peering down at me from the top floor. Black hair and eyes, set against the porcelain skin of an antique doll. Miles. He stared at me for a solemn moment, then disappeared again. That kid matched the original house perfectly.

Susan pulled down a tasteful print on the landing, so I could see the full wall.

"Here. It was right here." She pointed from the ceiling to the floor.

I pretended to examine it closely, but there was nothing really to see. She'd scrubbed it down completely; I could still smell the bleach.

"I can help you," I said. "There is a tremendous feeling of pain, right here. Throughout the whole house, but definitely here. I can help you."

"The house creaks all night long," she said. "I mean, it almost moans. It shouldn't. Everything inside is new. Miles's door slams at strange times. And he . . . he's getting worse. It's like something has settled on him. A darkness he carries on his back. Like an insect shell. He scuttles. Like a beetle. I'd move, that's how scared I am, I'd move, but we don't have the money. Anymore. We spent so much on this house, and then almost that much renovating, and . . . my husband won't let me anyway. He says Miles is just going through growing pains. And that I'm a nervous, silly woman."

"I can help you," I said.

"Let me give you the whole tour," she replied.

We walked down the long, narrow hall. The house was naturally dark. You moved away from a window and the gloom descended. Susan flipped on lights as we walked.

"Miles turns them off," she said. "Then I turn them back on. When I ask him to keep them on, he pretends he has no idea what I'm talking about.

Here's our den," she said. She opened a door to reveal a cavernous room with a fireplace and wall-to-wall bookshelves.

"It's a *library*," I gasped. They had to own a thousand books, easy. Thick, impressive, smart-people books. How do you keep a thousand books in one room and then call the room a den?

I stepped inside. I shivered dramatically. "Do you feel this? Do you feel the . . . heaviness here?"

"I hate this room." She nodded.

"I'll need to pay extra attention to this room," I said. I'd park myself in it for an hour at a time and just read, read whatever I wanted.

We went back into the hall, which was now dark again. Susan sighed and began flipping on lights. I could hear a patter of feet upstairs, running manically up and down the hallway. We passed a closed door to my right. Susan knocked at it—*Jack, it's me*. A shuffle of a chair being pushed back, a snick of a lock, and then the door was opened by another child, younger than Miles by several years. He looked like his mother. He smiled at Susan like he hadn't seen her in a year.

"Hi, Momma," he said. He wrapped his arms around her. "I missed you."

"This is Jack, he's seven," she said. She ruffled his hair.

"Momma has to go do a little work with her friend here," Susan said, kneeling to his eye level. "Finish your reading and then I'll make a snack."

"Do I lock the door?" Jack asked.

"Yes, always lock your door, sweetheart."

We started walking again as we heard the snick of the lock behind us.

"Why the lock?"

"Miles doesn't like his brother."

She must have felt my frown: No teenager likes his kid brother.

"You should see what Miles did to the babysitter he didn't like. It's one of the reasons we don't have money. Medical bills." She turned to me sharply. "I shouldn't have said that. It wasn't . . . major. Possibly an accident. I don't know anymore, actually. Maybe I am just goddamn crazy."

Her laugh was raw. She swiped at an eye.

We walked to the end of the hallway, where another door was locked.

"I'd show you Miles's room, but I don't have a key," she said simply. "Also, I'm too scared."

She forced another laugh. It wasn't convincing; it didn't have enough energy to even pose as a laugh. We went up to the next floor, which was a series of rooms, wallpapered and painted, with fine-boned Victorian furniture arranged haphazardly. One room held only a litterbox. "For our cat, Wilkie," Susan said. "Luckiest cat in the world: his own room for his own crap."

"You'll find a use for the space."

"He's actually a sweet cat," she said. "Almost twenty years old."

I smiled like that was interesting and good.

"We obviously have more room than we need," Susan said. "I think we thought, there might be another . . . maybe adopt, but I wouldn't bring another child into this house. So instead we live in a very expensive storage facility. My husband does like his antiques." I could picture him, this uptight, snooty husband. A man who bought antiques but didn't find them himself. Probably had some classy decorator woman in horn-rims doing the actual work. She probably bought those books for him too. I heard you could do that—buy books by the yard, turn them into furniture. People are dumb. I'll never get over how dumb people are.

We climbed some more. The top floor was just a large attic space with a few old steamer trunks all along the walls.

"Aren't the trunks stupid?" she whispered. "He says it gives the place a little authenticity. He didn't like the renovation."

So the house had been a compromise: The husband wanted vintage, Susan wanted new, so they thought this outside/inside split might settle things. But the Burkes ended up more resentful than satisfied. Millions of dollars later, and neither of them were happy. Money is wasted on the rich.

We went down the back stairs, cramped and dizzying, like an animal's burrow, and ended up in the gaping, gleaming modern kitchen.

Miles sat at the kitchen island, waiting. Susan started when she saw him.

He was small for his age. Pale face and pointy chin, and black eyes that reflected twitchily, like a spider's. Assessing. *Extremely bright but hates school*, I thought. *Never gets enough attention—even if he got all of Susan's attention it still wouldn't be enough. Mean-spirited. Self-centered.*

"Hi, Momma," he said. His face was transformed, a bright, goofy smile cracking through it. "I missed you." *Sweet-natured, loving Jack*. He was doing a perfect version of his little brother. Miles went to hug Susan, and as he walked, he assumed Jack's slump-shouldered, childish posture. He wrapped his arms around her, nuzzled into her. Susan watched me over his head, her cheeks flush, her lips tight as if she smelled something nasty. Miles gazed up at her. "Why won't you hug me?"

She gave him a brief hug. Miles released her as if he were scalded.

"I heard what you told her," he said. "About Jack. About the babysitter. About everything. You're such a bitch."

Susan flinched. Miles turned to me.

"I really hope you leave and don't come back. For your own good." He smiled at both of us. "This is a family matter. Don't you think, Momma?"

Then he was clattering in his heavy leather shoes up the back stairway again, leaning heavily forward. He did scuttle as if he bore an insect's shell, shiny and hard.

Susan looked at the floor, took a breath, and looked up. "I want your help."

"What does your husband say about all this?"

"We don't talk about it. Miles is his kid. He's protective. Anytime I say anything remotely critical, he says I'm crazy. He says I'm crazy a lot. A haunted house. Maybe I am. Anyway, he travels all the time; he won't even know you're here."

"I can help you," I said. "Shall we talk pricing very quickly?"

She agreed to the money, but not the timeline: "I can't wait a year for Miles to get better; he may kill us all before then." She gave that desperate burp of a laugh. I agreed to come twice a week.

Mostly I came during the day, when the kids were at school and Susan was at work. I did cleanse the house, in that I washed it. I lit my sage and sprinkled my sea salt. I boiled my lavender and rosemary, and I wiped down that house, walls and floors. And then I sat in the library and read. Also, I nosed around. I could find a zillion photos of grinning-sunshine Jack, a few old ones of pouty Miles, a couple of somber Susan and none of her husband. I felt sorry for Susan. An angry stepson and a husband who was always away, no wonder she let her mind go to dark places.

And yet. And yet, I felt it too: the house. Not necessarily malevolent, but . . . mindful. I could feel it studying me, does that makes sense? It crowded me. One day, I was wiping down the floorboards, and suffered a sudden, slicing pain in my middle finger—as if I'd been bitten—and when I pulled it away, I was bleeding. I wrapped my finger tightly in one of my spare rags and watched the blood seep through. And I felt like something in the house was pleased.

I began dreading. I made myself fight the dread. *You are the one who made this whole thing up*, I told myself. *So cut it out.*

Six weeks in, and I was boiling my lavender in the kitchen one morning—Susan off to work, the kids at school—when I felt a presence behind me. I turned to find Miles in his school uniform, examining me, a small smirk on his face. He was holding my copy of *The Turn of the Screw*.

"You like ghost stories?" He smiled.

He'd been through my purse.

"Why are you at home, Miles?"

"I've been studying you. You're interesting. You know something bad is going to happen, right? I'm curious."

He moved closer, I moved away. He stood next

to the pot of boiling water. His cheeks flushed from the heat.

"I'm trying to help, Miles."

"But you agree? You feel it? Evil?"

"I feel it."

He stared into the pot of water. Traced a finger on its edge, then snatched the finger away, pink. He assessed me with his shining black spider eyes.

"You don't look how I thought you'd look. Up close. I thought you'd be . . . *sexy*." He said the word ironically, and I knew what he meant: Halloween fortune-teller sexy. Lip gloss and big hair and hoop earrings. "You look like a babysitter."

I stepped farther back from him. He hurt the last babysitter.

"Are you trying to scare me, Miles?"

I wished I could reach the stove, turn off the burner.

"I'm trying to help you," he said reasonably. "I don't want you around her. If you come back, you will die. I don't want to say more than that. But I've warned you."

He turned away and left the room. When I heard him hit the front stairs, I poured the scalding water down the drain, then ran to the dining room to grab my purse, my keys. I needed to leave. When I picked up my purse, a foul, sweet heat hit my nostrils. He'd vomited inside—all over my keys and wallet and phone. I couldn't bear to pick up the keys, touch that sickness.

Susan banged through the door, frantic.

"Is he here? Are you OK?" she said. "School called, said Miles never showed. He must have walked in the front door and straight out the back. He doesn't like it that you're here. Did he say anything to you?"

A loud smash came from upstairs. A wail. We ran up the stairs. In the hallway, hanging from a ceiling hook, was a tiny, primitive figure made of cloth. A face drawn in magic marker. A noose made from red thread. Screaming came from Miles's room at the end of the hall. *Nonoooooooo, you bitch, you bitch!*

We stood outside the door.

"Do you want to talk to him?" I asked.

"No," she said.

She turned back down the hall in tears. Plucked the figure from the light fixture.

"I thought this was me at first," Susan said, handing it to me. "But I don't have brown hair."

"I think it's me," I said.

"I'm so tired of being afraid," she murmured.

"I know."

"You don't," she said. "But you will."

Susan went to her room. I went to work. I swear I worked. I washed the house—every inch of wall and floor—with rosemary and lavender. I smudged the sage and said my magical words that were gibberish as Miles screamed and Susan cried in the rooms above me. Then I dumped everything from my vomit-smeared purse into the kitchen sink and ran water over it until it was clean.

As I was unlocking my car in the dusk, an older woman, well powdered and plump-cheeked, called out to me from down the block. She scurried over in the mist, a little smile on her face.

"I just want to thank you for what you are doing for this family," she said. "For helping little Miles. Thank you." And then she put her fingers to her lips and pantomimed locking them, and scurried away again before I could tell her I was doing absolutely nothing to help this family.

A week later, as I was killing time in my tiny apartment (one bedroom, fourteen books), I noticed something new. A stain, like a rusty tidal pool on the wall by my bed. It reminded me of my mother. Of my old life. All the transactions—this for that, that for this—and none of it had made any difference until now. Once the transaction was complete, my mind was a blank, awaiting the next transaction. But Susan Burke and her family, they stuck with me. Susan Burke and her family and that house.

I opened up my ancient laptop and did a search: Patrick Carterhook. A whir and a grind and finally up came a link to an article from a university English Department: Victorian True Crime: The Grisly Tale of the Patrick Carterhook Family.

The year is 1893, and department-store magnate Patrick Carterhook moves into his splendid Gilded Age mansion in the heart of the city with his lovely wife, Margaret, and their two sons, Robert and Chester. Robert was a troubled boy, much given to bullying schoolmates and harming neighborhood pets. At age twelve, he burnt down one of his father's warehouses and remained on scene to watch the wreckage. He endlessly tormented his quiet younger brother. By age fourteen, Robert proved unable to control himself. The Carterhooks chose to keep him away from society: In 1895 they locked him inside the mansion. He was never again to set foot outdoors. Robert steadily grew more violent in his gloomy, gilded prison. He smeared his family's belongings with his own excrement and vomit.

A nursemaid was sent to the hospital with unexplained bruises; she never returned. The cook, too, fled one winter morning. Rumors had it that she'd suffered third-degree burns from boiling water in a "kitchen mishap."

No one knows exactly what went on in that house the night of January 7, 1897, but the bloody results are indisputable. Patrick Carterhook was discovered stabbed to death in his bed; his body was pocked with 117 knife wounds. Patrick's wife, Margaret, was found struck down by an ax—still in her back—as she was fleeing up the stairs to the attic, and young Chester, age ten, was found drowned in a bathtub. Robert hanged himself from a beam in his room. He had apparently dressed up for the occasion: he wore a blue Sunday suit, covered in his parents' blood. It was still wet from drowning his little brother.

Beneath the story was a blurry ancient photo of the Carterhooks. Four formal unsmiling faces peering out from layers of Victorian ruffles. A slender man in his forties with an artfully pointed beard; a blond, petite woman with sad, piercing eyes so light they looked white. Two boys, the younger blond like his mother; the elder dark-haired, black-eyed with a slight smirk and his head tilted at a knowing angle. Miles. The elder boy looked like Miles. Not a perfect match, but the essence was exact: the smugness, the superiority, the threat.

Miles.

If you remove the bloody floorboards and water-stained tiles; if you destroy the beams that held Robert Carterhook's body, and you tear down the walls that absorbed the screams, do you take down the house? Can it be haunted if the actual guts—its internal organs—have been removed? Or does the nastiness linger in the air? That night I dreamt of a small figure opening the door to Susan's room, creeping across the floor as she slept, and standing calmly over her with a gleaming butcher knife borrowed from her million-dollar kitchen. The room smelled of sage and lavender.

I slept into the afternoon and woke in the darkness, in the middle of a thunderstorm. I stared at the ceiling until the sun set, then got dressed and drove over to Carterhook Manor. I left my useless herbs behind.

Susan opened the door with wet eyes. Her pale faced glowed from the gloom of the house.

"You *are* psychic," she whispered. "I was going to call you. It's gotten worse, it's not stopping," she said. She collapsed onto a sofa.

"Are Miles and Jack here?"

She nodded and pointed a finger up. "Miles told me last night, quite calmly, that he was going to kill us," she said. "And I actually worry . . . because . . . Wilkie . . ." She was crying again. "Oh, God."

A cat padded slowly into the room. Ribby and worn, an old tomcat. Susan pointed to it.

"Look what he did . . . to poor Wilkie!"

I looked again. At the cat's back haunches was

only a frayed tuft of fur. Miles had cut off the cat's tail.

"Susan, do you have a laptop? I need to show you something."

She led me up to the library, and over to the Victorian desk that was clearly her husband's. She clicked a switch and the fireplace whooshed on. She hit a key and the laptop glowed. I showed Susan the website and the story of the Carterhooks. I could feel her warm breath on my neck as she read.

I pointed at the photo: "Does Robert Carterhook remind you of anyone?"

Susan nodded as if in a trance. "What does it mean?"

The rain spattered at the black windowpanes. I longed for a bright blue day. The heaviness of the house was unbearable.

"Susan, I like you. I don't like many people. I want the best for your family. And I don't think it's me."

"What do you mean?"

"I mean, you need someone to *help* you. I can't

help. There is something wrong with this house. I think you should leave. I don't care what your husband says."

"But if we leave . . . Miles is still with us."

"Yes."

"Then . . . he'll be cured? If he leaves this house?"

"Susan, I don't know."

"What are you saying?"

"I'm saying you need more than me to fix this. I'm not qualified. I can't fix it. I think you need to leave tonight. Go to a hotel. Two rooms. Lock the adjoining door. And then . . . we'll figure it out. But all I can really do for you is be your friend."

Susan stood dizzily, holding her throat. She pushed back from me, murmured *excuse me*, and disappeared out the door. I waited. My wrist was throbbing again. I glanced around the book-filled room. No parties here for me. No referrals to rich, nervous friends. I was ruining my big chance; I gave her an answer she didn't want. But I felt, for once, decent. Not telling-myself-I-am decent, but just decent.

I saw Susan flicker past the door heading down the stairs. Then Miles swooped immediately after her.

"Susan!" I yelled. I stood up but I couldn't will myself to go outside the room. I heard murmuring. Urgent or angry. Then nothing. Silence. And still nothing. *Go out there.* But I was too afraid to go alone into that dark hallway.

"Susan!"

A child who terrorized his little brother and threatened his stepmom. Who told me calmly that I would die. A kid who cut the tail off the family pet. A house that attacked and manipulated its own inhabitants. A house that had already seen four deaths and wanted more. *Stay calm.* The hallway was still dark. No sign of Susan. I stood. I began walking to the door.

Miles suddenly appeared in the doorway, stiff and upright, in his school uniform, as always. He was blocking my exit.

"I told you not to ever come back here, and you came back—you came back again and again," he said. Reasonable. Like he was talking to a child being punished. "You know you're going to die, right?"

"Where's your stepmom, Miles?" I backed away. He walked toward me. He was a small kid, but he scared me. "What did you do with Susan?"

"You're still not understanding, are you?" he said. "Tonight is when we die."

"I'm sorry, Miles, I didn't mean to upset you."

He laughed then, his eyes crinkling up. Complete mirth.

"No, you misunderstand me. She's going to *kill you. Susan* is going to kill you and me. Look around this room. Do you think you're here by accident? Look closely. Look at the books closely."

I had looked at the books closely. Every time I cleansed in here, I looked at all the books, I coveted them. I pictured stealing one or two for my little book club with . . .

With Mike. My favorite client. Every book I

ever read with Mike over the past few years was here. *The Woman in White*, *The Turn of the Screw*, *The Haunting of Hill House*. I'd congratulated myself when I'd seen them—how clever I was to have read so many of these fancy-people library books. But I wasn't a well-read bookworm; I was just a dumb whore in the right library. Miles pulled out a photo from the desk drawer, a wedding photo. The summer sunset behind the bride and groom left them backlit, shrouded. Susan was gorgeous, a luscious, lively version of the woman I knew. The groom? I barely recognized the face, but I definitely knew the dick. I had been giving hand jobs to Susan's husband for two years.

Miles was watching me, his eyes squinting, a comedian waiting for the audience to get the joke.

"She's going to kill you, and I'm pretty sure she's going to kill me too," he said.

"What do you mean?"

"She's calling 911 downstairs right now. She told me to stall you. When she comes up, she's going to shoot you, and she's going to tell the cops one of two things. One: You are a con artist who claims she has psychic powers in order to prey on the emotionally vulnerable. You told Susan you could help her mentally unstable son—and she trusted you—but instead, all you've been doing is coming into the house and stealing from her. When she confronted you, you became violent, you shot me, she shot you in self-defense."

"I don't like that one. What's the other option?"

"You actually are legit. You really did believe that the house was haunting me. But it turned out I'm not haunted, I'm just a run-of-the-mill teen sociopath. You pushed me too hard, I killed you. She and I struggled with the gun, she shot me in self-defense."

"Why would she want to kill you?"

"She doesn't like me, she never has. I'm not her son. She tried to pack me off to my mom, but my mom has zero interest. Then she tried to ship me to boarding school but my dad said no. She definitely would like me dead. It's just how she is. It's how she makes her living: She defines and eliminates problems. She's practical in an evil way."

"But she seems so——"

"Mousy? No, she's not. She wanted you to think that. She's a beautiful, successful executive. She's a goddamn overdog. But you needed to feel like you were preying on someone weaker than you. That you had the upper hand. I mean, am I wrong? Isn't that your whole business? Manipulating the manipulatable?"

My mom and I played that game for a decade: dressing and acting the part of people to be pitied. I didn't see it coming the other way.

"She wants to kill me . . . because of your dad?"

"Susan Burke had the perfect marriage, and you ruined it. My dad's gone. He left."

"I'm sure a few . . . liaisons is not the reason your dad left."

"It's the reason she has chosen to believe in.

It's the problem she has defined and plans to eliminate."

"Does your dad know . . . I'm here?"

"Not yet—he really does travel all the time. But once my dad learns we're dead, hears Susan's story? Once she tells him about being so scared, and coming across the business card for the psychic in his copy of *Rebecca*, and desperately asking her to help . . . imagine that guilt. His kid is dead because he wanted a hand job. His wife was forced to defend her family and *kill* because he got a hand job. That horror and guilt—he'll never be able to make it up to her. Which is the point."

"That's how she found me? My business card?"

"Susan found the card. She thought it was odd. Fishy. My dad loves ghost stories, but he's the world's biggest skeptic—he'd never see a palm reader. Unless . . . she wasn't really a palm reader. She followed him. She made an appointment. And then you walked in from the backroom with his copy of *The Woman in White*, and she knew."

"She confides in you."

"At first I took it as a compliment," he said. "Then I realized she's trying to distract me. She told me about her plan to kill you so I wouldn't realize I was going to die too."

"Why not just shoot me in an alley one night?"

"Then my dad feels no pain. And if she's seen? No. She wanted to kill you here, where it looked like she was the victim. It's actually the easiest way to do it. So she made up that haunted-house story to lure you here. Carterhook Manor, so *scary*."

"But the Carterhooks? I read about them online."

"The Carterhooks are a fiction. I mean, they existed, I guess, but they didn't die like you think."

"I read about them!"

"You read about them because she wrote about them. It's the Internet. Do you know how easy it is to make a web page? And then make some links to it, and then have people find it and believe it and add it to their web pages? It's tremendously easy. Especially for someone like Susan."

"That photo, it looked like—"

"Ever been to a flea market—shoebox after shoebox of those old photos, buck apiece. It's not hard to find a kid that might look like me. Especially if you have a person who is willing to believe. A sucker. Like you."

"The bleeding wall?"

"She just told you that. Sets the mood. She knew you liked ghost stories. She wanted you to come, and to believe. She likes to fuck with people. She wanted you to befriend her, be worried about her, and then—bam!—have that moment of shock when you realized you were going to die, and you'd been scared of the wrong thing. Your *senses* betrayed you."

He smirked at me.

"Who cut off your cat's tail?"

"It's a Manx, dummy, they have no tails. Can I answer any other questions on the road? I'd rather not wait here to die."

"You want to come with me?"

"Let's see: leave with you or stay here and die. Yeah, I'd like to come with you. She's probably done with her call. She's probably at the bottom of the stairs. I already hooked up the fire ladder in my room."

Susan's heels clattered across the living room, toward the stairs. Moving fast. Calling my name.

"Please take me with you," he said. "Please. Just until my dad gets home. Please, I'm scared."

"What about Jack?"

"She likes Jack. She only wants us gone."

Susan's footsteps quicker now, closer.

We took the fire escape. It was quite dramatic.

We were in my car, driving away before I realized I didn't know where the hell I was driving. Miles's pale face reflected passing headlights like a sickly moon. Raindrops glided from his forehead down his cheeks and off his chin.

"Call your dad," I said.

"My dad's in Africa."

The rain was clattering against my tinny rooftop. Susan Burke (that magnificent con artist!) had infused me with such a fear of the house, I'd been insensible. Now I could think: A successful woman marries a rich man. They have a baby who's a real charmer. The life is good except for one thing: the weirdo stepson. I believed her when she said Miles had always been cold to her. I'm sure she was always cold to Miles. I'm sure she tried to get rid of him from the start. Someone as calculating as Susan Burke wouldn't want to raise the oddball, awkward kid of another woman. Susan and Mike muddle along, but soon her cruelty toward his firstborn infects their relationship. He turns away from her. Her touch chills him. He comes to see me. And keeps seeing me. We have just enough in common, with the books, he can trick himself into thinking it's a relationship of some sort. Things with Susan continue to disintegrate. He moves out. He leaves Miles behind because he's traveling overseas—as soon as he returns, he'll make arrangements. (This was pure guess, but the Mike I knew, who giggled when he came, he seemed like a guy who'd retrieve his kid.) Unfortunately, Susan discovers his secret and blames me for the destruction of her marriage. Imagine the rage, that a lowdown woman like me was *handling* her husband. And now she was stuck with a creepy kid she hated and a house she didn't like. How to solve the problem? She begins to plot. She lures me in. Miles warns me in his elliptical way, toying with me, enjoying the game for a bit. Susan tells the neighbors something vague—that I'm here to help poor little Miles—so that when the truth comes out—that I'm a former hooker and current grifter—she will seem wretched, pitiful, pathetic. And I will seem ruinous. It's the perfect way to commit murder.

Miles looked over at me with his huge moon face and smiled.

"You know you're basically now a kidnapper," he said.

"I guess we need to go to the police."

"We need to go to Chattanooga, Tennessee," he said, somewhat impatiently, as if I were backing out of a long-standing plan. "Bloodwillow is there this year. It's always overseas—this is the first time it's been in the United States since 1978."

"I have no idea what you're talking about."

"It's only the biggest supernatural convention in the world. Susan said I couldn't go. So you can take me. I thought you'd be happy—you love ghost stories. You can hit the highway if you take a left at the third light up there."

"I'm not taking you to Chattanooga."

"You'd better take me. I'm in charge now."

"You are delusional, little boy."

"And you are a thief and a kidnapper."

"I'm neither."

"Susan didn't call 911 because she was about to kill you." He laughed. "She called 911 because I told her I caught you stealing. She's been missing jewelry, you see." He patted the pockets of his blazer. I heard a jangle inside.

"By now she has come back upstairs and found her troubled stepson kidnapped by a fortune-telling hooker-thief. So we'll have to lie low for a few days. Which is fine, Bloodwillow doesn't start till Thursday."

"Susan wanted to kill me because she found out about me and your dad."

"You can say *hand job*, you know," he said. "It doesn't offend me."

"Susan found out."

"Susan found out nothing. She's an incredibly intelligent idiot. I figured it out. I borrow my dad's books all the time. *I* found your business card, *I* found your notes in the margins. *I* went to your place of work and figured it out. Part of what Susan said is true: She does think I'm weird. When we moved here—after I told her I didn't want to; I was very clear that I didn't want to— I started making things happen, in the house. Just to screw with her. *I* made up that website. Me. *I* made up the story of the Carterhooks. *I* sent her to you, just to see if she would finally freakin' figure it out and leave. She didn't, she fell for your bullshit."

"So Susan was telling the truth, about all the

scary things in the house. You really did threaten to kill your brother?"

"It says more about her that she believed me than it does about me that I said it."

"You really did throw your sitter down the stairs?"

"Please, she fell. I'm not violent, I'm just smart."

"That day, with the vomit in my purse and the fit you had upstairs and the doll hanging from the light?"

"The vomit was me because you weren't listening to me. You weren't leaving. The doll too. Also the razor-blade tip in the floorboard that sliced your finger. That's actually an idea inspired by ancient Roman warfare. Have you ever read—"

"No. The screaming you did? You sounded so furious."

"Oh, that was real. Susan had cut up my credit card and left it on my desk. She was trying to wall me in. But then I realized you were my way out of that stupid house. I need a grownup to do anything, really: drive a car, get a hotel room. I'm too little for my age. I'm fifteen but I look like I'm twelve. I need someone like you to really get around. All I had to do was get you to take me out of the house, and you were done. Because you know you're not going to show up at the cops. I assume someone like you has a criminal record."

Miles was right. People like me didn't go to the police, ever, because it never turned out well for us.

"Turn left up here to catch the freeway," he said.

I turned left.

I took in his story, turned it over, and inspected it. *Wait, wait.*

"Wait. Susan said you cut off your cat's tail. You told me it was a Manx . . ."

He smiled then.

"Ha! Good point. So someone's lying to you. I guess you'll have to decide which story to believe. Do you want to believe Susan is a nutjob or that

I'm a nutjob? Which would make you feel more comfortable? At first, I thought it'd be better if you thought Susan was the crazy—that you'd be sympathetic to my plight, and we'd be friends. Road-trip buddies. But then I thought: Maybe it's better if you think I'm the evil one. Maybe then you're more likely to understand I'm in charge here . . . what do you think?"

We drove in silence as I viewed my options.

Miles interrupted me. "I mean, I really think it's a win-win-win here. If Susan is the nutjob and she wants us gone, we're gone."

"What will she tell your dad when he gets home?"

"That depends on what story you want to believe."

"Is your dad really even in Africa?"

"I don't think my dad is a factor you need to worry about in your decision-making."

"OK, so what if you're the nutjob, Miles? Your mom will have the cops on us."

"Pull over at that parking lot, the church."

I looked him up and down for a weapon. I didn't want to be a body dumped in an abandoned church lot.

"Just do it, OK?" Miles snapped.

I pulled into a shuttered church parking lot just off the highway entrance. Miles leapt out in the rain and ran up the stairs and under the eaves. He pulled his cell from his blazer and made a call, his back to me. He was on the phone for a minute. Then he smashed the phone to the ground, stomped on it a few times, and ran back to the car. He smelled disturbingly springlike.

"OK, I just called my nervous little stepmom. I told her you freaked me out, I'm sick of the house and all her weirdness—her habit of bringing in such unsavory people—and so I ran off and I'm staying at my dad's place. He just got back from Africa and so I'll stay there. She never calls my dad."

And he smashed the phone so I couldn't see if he really called Susan or if he was just playacting again.

64

"And what will you tell your dad?"

"Let's just remember that when you have two parents who hate each other and are always working or traveling and would like you out of their lives anyway, you can say a lot of things. You have a lot of room to work with. So you really don't need to worry. Get to the highway and then there's a motel about three hours on. Cable TV and a restaurant."

I got on the highway. The kid was sharper at fifteen than I was at twice his age. I was starting to think this whole going legit, thinking-of-others, benevolent thing was *fer the berds*. I was starting to think this kid might be a good partner. This tiny teen needed a grownup to move in the world, and there was nothing a con girl could use more than a great con kid. "What do you do?" people would ask, and I'd say, "I'm a mom." Think of what I could get away with, the scams I could pull, if people thought I was a sweet little *mom*.

Plus that Bloodwillow convention sounded really cool.

We pulled into the motel three hours later, just as Miles had projected. We got adjoining rooms.

"Sleep tight," Miles said. "Don't leave in the night, or I'll call the cops and go back to the kidnap story. I promise that's the last time I'll threaten you, I don't want to be an asshole. But we've *got* to get to Chattanooga! We're going to have so much fun, I swear. I can't believe I'm going. I've wanted to go since I was seven!" He did a strange little dance of excitement and went into his room.

The kid was kind of likable. Also a possible sociopath, but very likable. I had a good feeling about him. I was going with a smart kid to a place where everyone wanted to talk about books. I was finally going to leave town for the first time in my life, and I had the whole new "mommy" angle to work. I decided not to worry: I may never know the truth about the happenings at Carterhook Manor (how's that for a great line?). But I was either screwed or not screwed, so I chose to believe I wasn't. I had convinced so many people of so many things over my life, but this would be my greatest feat: convincing myself what I was doing was reasonable. Not decent, but reasonable.

I got in bed and watched the door of the adjoining room. Checked the lock. Turned off the light. Stared at the ceiling. Stared at the adjoining door.

Pulled the dresser in front of the door.

Nothing to worry about at all.

Thanks to George R. R. Martin, who asked me
to write him a story.

Coming in 2016

DARK PLACES

A major motion picture by
Gilles Paquet-Brenner
Starring Charlize Theron

Read the book before you see the film

Available now in paperback and ebook

Libby Day was just seven years old when her evidence put her fifteen-year-old brother behind bars.

Since then, she has been drifting. But when she is contacted by a group who are convinced of Ben's innocence, Libby starts to ask questions she never dared to before. Was the voice she heard her brother's? Ben was a misfit in their small town, but was he capable of murder? Are there secrets to uncover at the family farm or is Libby deluding herself because she wants her brother back?

She begins to realise that everyone in her family had something to hide that day . . . especially Ben. Now, twenty-four years later, the truth is going to be even harder to find. Who did massacre the Day family?

Turn over for a chilling extract . . .

"So what's with the club?" I prompted.

Lyle turned pink, his knee jittery beneath the table.

"Well, you know how some guys do fantasy football, or collect baseball cards?" I nodded. He let out a strange laugh and continued. "Or women read gossip magazines and they know everything about some actor, know like, their baby's name and the town they grew up in?"

I gave a wary incline of the head, a be-careful nod.

"Well, this is like that, but it's, well, we call it a Kill Club."

I took a slug of beer, sweat beads popping on my nose.

"It's not as weird as it sounds."

"It sounds pretty fucking weird."

"You know how some people like mysteries? Or get totally into true-crime blogs? Well, this club is a bunch of those people. Everyone has their crime that they're obsessed with: Laci Peterson, Jeffrey MacDonald, Lizzie Borden . . . you and your family. I mean you and your family, it's huge with the club. Just huge. Bigger'n JonBenét." He caught me grimacing, and added: "Just a tragedy, what happened. And your brother in jail for, what, going on twenty-five years?"

"Don't feel sorry for Ben. He killed my family."

"Heh. Right." He sucked on a piece of milky ice. "So, you ever talk with him about it?"

I felt my defenses flip up. There are people out there who swear Ben is innocent. They mail me newspaper clippings about Ben and I never read them, toss them as soon as I see his photo—his red hair loose and shoulder-length in a Jesus-cut to match his glowing, full-of-peace face. Pushing forty. I have never gone to see my brother in jail, not in all these years. His current prison is, conveniently, on the outskirts of our hometown —Kinnakee, Kansas—where he'd committed the murders to begin with. But I'm not nostalgic.

Most of Ben's devotees are women. Jug-eared and long-toothed, permed and pant-suited, tight-lipped and crucifixed. They show up occasionally on my doorstep, with too much shine in their eyes. Tell me that my testimony was wrong. I'd been confused, been coerced, sold a lie when I swore, at age seven, that my brother had been the killer. They often scream at me, and they always have plenty of saliva. Several have actually slapped me. This makes them even less convincing: A redfaced, hysterical woman is very easy to disregard, and I'm always looking for a reason to disregard.

If they were nicer to me, they might have got me.

"No, I don't talk to Ben. If that's what this is about, I'm not interested."

"No, no, no, it's not. You'd just come to, it's like a convention almost, and you'd let us pick your brain. You really don't think about that night?"

Darkplace.

"No, I don't."

"You might learn something interesting. There are some fans . . . experts, who know more than the detectives on the case. Not that *that's* hard."

"So these are a bunch of people who want to convince me Ben's innocent."

"Well . . . maybe. Maybe you'll convince them otherwise." I caught a whiff of condescension. He was leaning in, his shoulders tense, excited.

"I want $1,000."

"I could give you $700."

I glanced around the room again, noncommittal. I'd take whatever Lyle Wirth gave me, because otherwise I was looking at a real job, real soon, and

I wasn't up for that. I'm not someone who can be depended on five days a week. Monday Tuesday Wednesday Thursday Friday? I don't even get out of bed five days in a row—I often don't remember to eat five days in a row. Reporting to a workplace, where I would need to stay for eight hours—eight big hours outside my home—was unfeasible.

"Seven hundred's fine then," I said.

"Excellent. And there'll be a lot of collectors there, so bring any souvenirs, uh, items from your childhood you might want to sell. You could leave with $2,000, easy. Letters especially. The more personal the better, obviously. Anything dated near the murders. January 3, 1985." He recited it as if he'd said it often. "Anything from your mom. People are really . . . fascinated by your mom."

People always were. They always wanted to know: What kind of woman gets slaughtered by her own son?